PIP

THE ADVENTURES
OF A
DEER MOUSE

PIP
THE ADVENTURES
OF A
DEER MOUSE

SHIRLEY E. WOODS

illustrations by
BRUCE JOHN WOOD

NIMBUS
PUBLISHING

Nimbus Publishing Limited
P.O. Box 9301, Station A
Halifax, Nova Scotia
B3K 5N5

Design: John Colville, Halifax

Canadian Cataloguing in Publication Data

Woods, Shirley E.

Pip

ISBN 0-91054-98-X

I. Title.

PS8595.063P56 1991 JC813'.54 C91-097640-6 PZ10.3.W66Pi 1991

Printed and bound in Canada

TABLE OF CONTENTS

*This book is affectionately dedicated to Amy and Jasmine,
and, of course, to my own Pip and Meg.*

ONE

A Mouse Is Born

P ip was born in an old army boot on an abandoned farm in Saskatchewan. It was a warm, lilac-scented spring morning. At the moment of his birth a bluebird burst into song. Pip's mother was delighted. To be welcomed into the world by a bluebird was a lucky omen.

Pip was the oldest in his litter. He and his three sisters—Amy, Beth, and Jasmine—were born without fur and looked like pink jelly beans with stubby tails. Unable to hear or see, they were totally dependent on their mother. She fed them with her milk, washed them with her tongue, and protected them with her body.

Their home was hidden in a field of tall, thick grass close to a tumble-down fence. Pip's mother had managed to make a snug nest inside the toe of the old boot. Shafts of light filtered down the entrance and through the lace holes, and a tear in the toe cap, which had once glistened with polish, served as a window.

Pip's eyes and ears opened when he was two weeks old. By now he no longer looked like a jelly bean but a young deer mouse. His body was bigger, his tail was longer, and he had a velvety coat that was slate grey along his back and white on his stomach.

Being able to see was a thrill for Pip and his sisters. Filled with awe, they examined each other and their surroundings. Pip nuzzled his mother, played with his sisters, and explored every part of the den. He was the most curious of the baby mice. He even climbed the tongue of the boot and peeked through an eyelet at the

1

gigantic sky. There was so much to see and so much to discover.

Soon Pip's curiosity drew him out of the nest into the field. Within minutes he was lost. Cowering under the stalks of grass, which seemed as tall as trees, he cried for his mother. She quickly found him and, after scolding him, led him home. Pip's sisters, who had anxiously watched him go, greeted him with happy squeaks.

One moonlit night a coyote pup discovered the mice's den. Drawn by their odour, he scraped at the boot, rocking it with his paw. Inside, Pip's mother shivered with fear while her babies slept, unaware of the danger.

They were saved by a hare crouched under a nearby bush. When the hare heard the scratching sound, it bolted from its hiding place. In an instant the coyote forgot about the mice and pelted after the hare.

But Pip's mother knew the coyote would return, so just before dawn she moved her family. Carrying the mice one at a time in her mouth, with their heads and tails wrapped around her throat like a scarf, she took them to a place where she had stayed the previous autumn. When the sun came up, her babies were safe in their new home, a nest of grass in the middle of a hayfield.

That evening Pip's father visited the family. This was a pleasant surprise. Male deer mice don't live with their families and rarely—sometimes never—see their little ones. Pip's father had shiny black whiskers, large grey ears, and a long sleek tail. His dense coat was light brown above and white below, just like a deer's. After touching noses with Pip's mother, he played with his babies for a few minutes and then disappeared into the night.

The next day Pip, as curious as ever, slipped out of the nest again. This time he shinnied up a goldenrod plant and then, when he was as high as he dared go, held himself up by wrapping his tail around the stem. From his perch near the top of the weed

he could see in every direction. While he proudly surveyed the vast expanse of grass, a bumblebee buzzed past him. Pip watched the bee and thought, "What fun it would be to fly!"

When he finally arrived home, his mother was very upset. She sat him down and told him sternly, "Pip, we have many enemies, and going out alone was a very dangerous thing to do. From now on you must not leave the nest without me." Softening her tone, she added, "Soon enough you'll be on your own."

As the days sped by, Pip and his sisters grew stronger and more agile. Gradually their mother reversed their routine so that they slept or rested during the day and stayed awake at night.

When they were a month old, their mother weaned them from milk to solid food. She took the young mice on nightly journeys and fed them seeds, berries, and bugs. Seeds were abundant, and wild strawberries grew in little patches on the edge of the hayfield. Pip loved strawberries, and he ate them with such gusto that the juice stained his cheeks and dribbled off his whiskers. He also liked beetles, June bugs, and caterpillars. When he was thirsty, he drank from a puddle or lapped the dew off the grass.

Pip's second month was busy and exciting. Each night he and his sisters followed their mother along the secret mouse paths to feed and to learn the lay of the land. Rambling in the dark, Pip had to rely on all his senses. His shoe-button eyes saw well at night, and his nose could pick up messages from the slightest breeze. In confined places, such as underground tunnels, he often used his sensitive whiskers to probe his way through. His big ears, like radar dishes that tuned into distant sounds, were his early-warning system.

Pip's mother constantly warned the young mice to be on the alert for danger. But Pip thought she was being overly cautious and didn't pay much attention … until one night he saw a black form, silent as a shadow, slide across the moon. For a moment he

4

froze with fear, and then he started to run. He'd taken only a few steps when an owl swooped out of the darkness and nearly caught him. This terrifying experience taught Pip a lesson that he never forgot. From then on he kept his eyes and ears open, and he was extra careful.

His vigilance was rewarded a few nights later. The family was walking in single file along the edge of a meadow when Pip heard a twig snap in the distance. He squeaked a warning, and all the family took cover. Trembling, they watched a fox emerge from the bushes and pad quietly past their hiding place. Had it not been for Pip's keen ears, the fox might have had them for supper.

On a warm afternoon in July, while they were dozing in their den, Pip's mother drew him aside and said, "You're two months old now, Pip. It's time for you to leave the nest and make your own way in the world."

Pip was terrified at the thought and started to protest. "But ... but ... why ... where—"

"I'm very sorry," his mother interrupted, "you must go because I'm expecting another litter of babies soon. Your sisters will help me for a few weeks, and then they too will have to leave."

That evening Pip said goodbye to his family and set off in the gathering dusk. As he was leaving, his mother tried to console him. "You're going to be all right," she said. "Remember, a bluebird sang when you were born, and that means luck will always be with you." Trudging across the field, Pip didn't feel at all lucky. He just felt sad. He thought about all the fun he had had with his sisters and about how much he would miss his mother. By the time he reached the fence, he was feeling very sorry for himself. Here, as chance would have it, he met his father.

"Mom says I must leave," Pip cried, "but I don't know where to go. It's so unfair."

"It seems unfair, Pip," his father said, "but it's part of growing up. You can come with me tonight, and we'll look for a new home for you."

This lifted Pip's spirits. Together, they explored the next field to find a place for Pip to live. Eventually they chose a ground squirrel's abandoned burrow. It had a small entrance and a hidden exit—it wasn't perfect, but it would do. Pip's father helped remove the rotted vegetation that the squirrel had used to line his sleeping chamber, and then the two mice cut fresh grass with their sharp front teeth and carried bundles of it in their mouths to Pip's new home.

By the time they finished gathering grass, the sky was growing pink in the east. Knowing that hawks would soon be on the wing, they hurried to Pip's father's den.

During the first few days that Pip lived by himself, he stayed close to his burrow and went out only for a few hours each night.

His new home was quite comfortable, but he was lonely and he longed to see his mother and sisters. Finally he became so homesick that he decided to pay them a visit.

As he was scrambling under the fence into their hayfield, he caught a strange scent and heard human voices. Pip had never seen a human, although he had been warned by his mother to avoid them. Torn between curiosity and fear, he crept forward. Taking a deep breath, he peered over the grass. Two huge figures were standing in the field. The sight of the men gave Pip such a fright that he decided to postpone his visit to the following night.

At sunup the next morning Pip heard the rumble of machinery. The noise sounded as though it was coming from the field where his mother and sisters lived. Pip couldn't see what was going on, but he sensed his family was in peril. The machinery clattered and clanked all day. An hour before sunset a tractor towed the mower from the field, and the rumbling gradually faded in the distance.

As soon as it was dark, Pip set off to see his family. He didn't stop to eat along the way, and he took several shortcuts. He was worried that something dreadful had happened to the field where his family lived. And if something bad had happened to the field, then what about his family? He shuddered just thinking about it.

When Pip reached the fence, he was almost too scared to look.

What he saw confirmed his worst fears.

The field, which had been a rippling sea of tall grass, was now bare stubble. Frantically Pip ran over to where his family's nest had been. There was no sign of it. Then he ran to the far side, where his father's den had been, but it too had vanished.

Crouching in the stubble, his tail twitching, Pip tried to gather his wits. Slowly and painfully he realized that his family was gone.

He was alone in the world.

TWO

EASTWARD BOUND

Pip was heartbroken at the loss of his family. For several days he stayed in his den, rolled up in a sad little ball. He hardly moved, and he ate nothing. He seemed to be in a trance.

Little by little, Pip began to feel better. By the evening of the third day he was nearly his old self. As soon as it was dark, he left his burrow in search of food. He was starving! The first thing he found was a fat beetle, which he crunched with relish. His next course was a hearty helping of clover seeds. Then he came upon a long green caterpillar. Just as he was about to capture this delicacy, he noticed a flicker of movement in the grass. His senses alerted, he stared at the spot.

The grass parted and, to Pip's surprise, into the clearing hopped a young mouse.

For one joyous moment Pip thought it was his sister Amy, but his spirits sank when he realized it was a stranger. Pip and the stranger confronted each other, their ears folded back, their whiskers twitching nervously. Both were ready to flee but at the same time anxious to meet. The two mice edged closer. Gingerly they touched noses and sniffed each other's cheeks.

The stranger broke the silence. "You don't seem very happy," he said.

"I'm not." Pip sighed. "I miss my parents and my sisters. Some humans destroyed their homes, and now I'm an orphan."

Pip's new acquaintance was named Toby, and as it turned out, he was the same age. Toby, too, had been forced by his mother to leave the nest. But he wasn't at all homesick. When he and Pip met, he had been on his way to the grain elevator to eat wheat.

"Why don't you come along, Pip?" Toby asked. "There's plenty of grain for both of us, and it's not far from here."

"I don't know," Pip said uncertainly. "My father warned me to stay away from there because of the guard cats."

"Oh, come on. You've got to take a chance some time. Besides, grain tastes better than weed seeds!"

Pip wasn't very hungry any more, but he was lonely, so he agreed to go.

The grain elevator was a tall wooden building by the railway tracks, on the outskirts of town. A huge freight train with endless cars fading into the darkness stood opposite the elevator. When Pip and Toby arrived, it was midnight, and the whole place was deserted and eerily silent.

Waving his paw like a magician, Toby showed Pip where the grain was funnelled into the railcars. Then he pointed to a pile of kernels beside the track. The two mice scampered over and began their meal.

They fed shoulder to shoulder at first, but after finishing the seeds, they went their separate ways. Pip followed a sparse trail of wheat and eventually found himself beneath the door of a boxcar. Glancing up, he noticed the door was open a crack.

Pip and Toby didn't know it, but they were being watched by a pair of unblinking yellow eyes. It was Tombo, the guard cat. Tombo had caught hundreds and hundreds of mice, and his name struck terror in the mouse community. As soon as Pip and Toby split up, the big black tomcat began his deadly stalk. His gaze penetrating the darkness, he moved slowly without making a sound. He had already selected his first victim.

When Pip put his head down to pick up another mouthful,

Tombo eased into position to pounce. Then the cat bunched his muscles and sprang.

Pip saw Tombo out of the corner of his eye. In a single bound the young mouse vaulted onto the ladder and slipped through the door of the boxcar. With a yowl of rage, Tombo flung himself at the door, but the opening was much too narrow. Pip was safe.

His heart pounding, Pip watched the opening intently. Outside, it was ghostly quiet. The minutes dragged by, and still nothing happened. Gathering his courage, he crept to the door and looked out. Both Toby and the cat had disappeared.

Just as Pip was about to jump to the ground, his sixth sense told him something was wrong. He scanned the loading area a second time but saw nothing that aroused his suspicion. Then he noticed a shadow near the ladder. Tombo was waiting for him!

Pip knew he must find another way out. Standing on his hind legs, he surveyed the empty boxcar. The floor and walls were solid wood, there were no windows, and the other door was sealed shut. He was trapped.

He scurried back and forth desperately, looking for a hiding place. But he couldn't find one. Then he noticed a chink at the base of the far wall where a piece of wood had broken off. Poking his nose into the hole, he discovered a space between the inner wood wall and the outer steel shell of the car. It was dusty and dark, but it would serve as a temporary refuge.

Pip squeezed through the chink, brushed aside a spider web, and cleared a space for himself. He was so tired from all the excitement that he tucked his head into his stomach, curled his tail around his feet, and fell fast asleep.

The sounds of men talking and gravel crunching woke him. The voices and steps drew nearer, and then they were right outside. With a clang, someone threw open the door of the boxcar. Sunlight flooded the car, illuminating the entrance to

Pip's shelter, and two men appeared at the doorway. One of them climbed in—and a few seconds later, so did Tombo, the guard cat!

Tombo slinked towards the opening of Pip's hideaway. He hissed and scratched at the chink in the wall. Pressed into a corner, Pip could do nothing but stare at the cat in horror.

Finally the man in the boxcar grabbed the cat by the scruff of the neck and swung him to the ground. "Out of here, Tombo! It's your job to watch the elevator, it's our job to inspect the railway cars!"

Two large boots clumped towards Pip's hideout. But to his relief, they stopped short and retreated. As the man hopped to the ground, he said to his companion, "We won't load this car. It hasn't been cleaned properly, and the latch on the door is broken."

When the men left, they shut the door. Once again it was pitch dark.

Suddenly Pip heard a distant whistle and felt the boxcar jolt forward. The floor shuddered beneath him, and the wheels began to grind. The train was moving!

As the train gained speed, the clatter rose to a roar. *Clickety clack! Clickety clack! Clickety clack!* The boxcar shook so violently that Pip was sure it would fly apart. But the only thing that moved was the door with the broken latch. It slid open a crack.

Gradually the racket died down and the pitching turned into a gentle sway. Lulled by the steady rhythm of the wheels, Pip began to relax. Wherever he was bound, he had a hiding place and lots of food—dead flies and spiders, as well as grain that had spilled between the walls.

The hours passed as the train chugged steadily eastward. *Clickety clack. Clickety clack. Clickety clack.*

The next morning Pip noticed a tangy scent in the air. Curious, he walked to the door and looked out. A dense forest of evergreens stretched to the horizon. He had never seen country like this before, and he was fascinated by how wild and green it looked—how different it was from his golden prairie home.

But the scenery held Pip's attention for only a moment. He was growing thirstier by the second, and there wasn't a drop of water in the boxcar. To make matters worse, it was now stifling hot, and there was a haze of dust in the car.

Hours later, feeling miserable, Pip went back to the door for a breath of fresh air. Heavy black clouds were massing overhead. Suddenly a bolt of lightning split the sky. Then, over the clatter of the train, Pip heard the crash of thunder. It was going to rain!

The rain fell in torrents. Pip listened happily as it drummed on the shell of the boxcar. To his relief, some drops splashed through the opening and formed a puddle on the floor. Scampering over to the puddle, he drank and drank.

The storm cleared the air and cooled the interior of the car. For the first time that day Pip felt comfortable. Then he started thinking. Where was he going? What would happen when he got there? These questions kept nagging him, and he knew that only time would reveal the answers.

In the middle of the night the train pulled into the freight yards of a large city. Pip listened to the sounds of activity outside. A clang here, the roar of an engine there. Several people passed his car, but no one came in. Finally the train moved to the outskirts of the yard.

Soon someone did approach Pip's boxcar. The man stopped, eased the door open, and climbed in.

He closed the door quietly and slumped against the rear wall. Mumbling to himself, he rummaged in his pockets. A match flared as he lit a cigarette, and a foul burning smell floated through the air, stinging Pip's nostrils. The cigarette glowed like a

red eye until it burned to a stub the man could no longer hold. With a sigh, he ground the butt into the floor, pulled his tattered coat around him, and rolled over and went to sleep.

Without warning, the train started to move. *Clickety clack! Clickety clack! Clickety clack!*

Cautiously Pip emerged from the wall. Just as he started towards the man, a loud snore sent Pip scurrying back into his den. A few minutes went by, and the man didn't stir or make a sound, so Pip decided to try again. This time he was able to tiptoe around the sleeping figure. Pip sniffed and studied him from all angles. His hair was untidy, and his glasses had slipped halfway down his nose. Each time he drew a breath, his long grey whiskers rippled like a field of grain. "This human seems harmless," Pip thought to himself.

Early the next morning, while the man was still sleeping, Pip crept over to the door for a drink. To his dismay he noticed the puddle was almost gone. As he was lapping the last drops, the man stirred and sat up. Pip froze, and for an instant their eyes met.

"Hi, little fellah! It's nice to see ya! I thought I was the only one in this boxcar, an' I was gettin' pretty lonely!"

The man stretched out his hand. But the sound of his voice and his friendly gesture terrified the young mouse, and he bolted for his refuge. "Aw, I'm sorry, little fellah," the man cried. "I didn't mean to scare ya."

It was a long and tedious day. Crouched in his nook, Pip was hot, and the dust made him sneeze. But he didn't dare leave the safety of his den.

That afternoon the train stopped briefly at a rail junction. Pip and his fellow stowaway listened intently to the clanking sounds of the cars being checked. As voices drew closer, the man stood up. Suddenly he shoved the door open and jumped out. Shouts followed his retreating steps, and moments later a railway policeman appeared at the opening and looked inside the car. Satisfied that no one else was there, he slammed the door shut with an oath.

When the train started, the door slid open again. Peering through the crack, Pip saw that the countryside had changed once more. Unbroken forest had given way to scattered woodlots and rolling farmland.

Too thirsty to eat, Pip dozed fitfully in his den, dreaming of dew-laden grass and juicy berries. That night he paced restlessly.

The boxcar was no longer a refuge but a prison.

THREE

A New Home

A shaft of sunlight on the floor foretold another hot day. Pip didn't know how he would get through it. His throat was so dry that he found it impossible to sleep.

Around mid-afternoon the train halted at a railway crossing. Although he was feeling weak and light-headed, Pip was drawn to the door by the sweet scent of water. Below the track was a sparkling brook.

In a flash he made up his mind. Without a backwards glance, Pip leaped from the boxcar to the embankment. He landed on loose gravel and tumbled down the bank. Unhurt, he righted himself and shook the dust from his fur. His journey was over.

He didn't know it, but he had travelled all the way from the Prairies to the Atlantic coast.

Frantic for water, he scrambled down the slope to the stream. Wading up to his belly, he drank deeply. The train gave a mournful hoot and started to move, but Pip paid no attention to the commotion. By the time he looked up, the train had chugged out of sight.

Standing at the edge of the brook, he studied the countryside. Behind him was the bare gravel embankment. In front of him was open woodland. Because the forest promised both food and shelter, Pip decided to go there.

This posed a problem. To get to the woods, he had to cross the brook.

Pip had never swum before. But his instincts told him that if he walked into the water and kept his legs moving, he would stay afloat. Gingerly he tested his theory in a quiet backwater. It worked! He could swim!

Just as he was about to wade into the stream, he heard a violent splash beneath a tree that overhung the far bank. Startled, Pip said aloud, "What was that?"

To his surprise a dragonfly hovering nearby replied. "That was Trutta the Brown Trout. She just caught a minnow." As he darted away in a blur of gossamer wings, the dragonfly whispered: "If you swim through the pool, you'd better watch out, or she'll eat you, too!"

Pip heeded the warning and walked well upstream from the trout's lair. Quietly he slipped into the brook and started for the opposite shore, kicking his hind legs and paddling with his forefeet. Ears folded back, he kept his head out of the water and used his tail as a rudder. It was easy going until the surface became rippled and he was buffeted by tiny waves. Bobbing up and down, he was frightened, but he pressed on.

In midstream Pip was hit by the full force of the current. No matter how hard he kicked, he couldn't make any headway. Slowly, then faster and faster, he was dragged downstream. A rock loomed in his path, and he shut his eyes. Fortunately the current curved around the rock, and Pip swept past it. Then, with a *whoosh*, he shot down a rapid into a quiet pool.

For a few moments Pip treaded water. The pool looked familiar. There was the tree, and there was Trutta, still feeding. Pip was back where he had started. As he watched, a mayfly glided under the branches like a miniature sailboat and disappeared with a splash.

Fearing he would be the trout's next victim, Pip paddled furiously for the shore. But just before he reached the bank, he saw a glimmer of gold in the water.

Trutta's glistening back broke the surface right behind him. Pip felt a searing pain in his tail, and the next thing he knew, he was being pulled under the water. He panicked and squirmed to get away, but trailing a necklace of bubbles, he went down and down.

Just when he thought his lungs would burst, Pip pulled free and popped to the surface like a cork. Gasping and spluttering, he saw he was within a few strokes of the bank. Terrified that Trutta would attack again, he summoned the last of his strength and swam to safety. He hauled himself out of the water, staggered into a crevice in the rocks, and collapsed.

When Pip came to, the sun was casting long shadows. He looked around warily, sniffed the breeze, and listened for hostile sounds. Then he crept into a patch of flickering sunlight to groom himself. He was a mess.

Pip began the ritual by licking his forepaws. This done, he smoothed the fur on his face with his forepaws, stroking from his nose to behind his ears. Then, using his nails as combs, with a lick here and a nibble there, he cleaned his body and legs. Finally, he grasped his tail and ran it through his mouth from the base to the tip. It still smarted. Near the tip were several needlelike scratches from Trutta's sharp teeth.

Pip felt much better after sprucing himself up. The brook was no longer a fearsome obstacle but a shiny ribbon that gurgled peacefully in the fading light. In the distance a robin saluted the end of the day. "Cheer up! Cheer up!" she sang. Then a kingfisher flashed by with a harsh rattle, disappearing upstream in a patch of blue.

Pip turned his mind to practical matters—he had to find something to eat. This was easy. Wherever he looked, there was

food. Sedge grass overflowing with seeds bordered the stream bank, clumps of goldenrod stood only a few steps away, and a raspberry bush full of ripe fruit beckoned nearby. Pip snacked on grass seeds and goldenrod as he made his way to a feast of raspberries.

While he was nibbling on a berry, a mouselike creature approached the bush. The newcomer was about Pip's size, with a buff-grey coat and a light stomach. But his head, ears, legs, and tail were all shorter than a mouse's. When he spotted Pip, he stopped and stared at him.

"A deer mouse, you're a deer mouse, aren't you?" the stranger asked.

"Yes," Pip answered timidly. "What are you?"

"A red-backed vole, I'm a red-backed vole." With that, the vole turned around to show off the chestnut stripe that ran from his forehead to his tail. "Friends call me The Gapper, or sometimes just plain Gapper."

"I'm happy to meet you, Mr. Gapper. I don't know anyone here. You're the first animal I've met."

"Well, that's lucky for you, lucky indeed. If you'd met Chark the Short-tailed Shrew, it wouldn't have been so nice! Do you know what a short-tailed shrew is? Eh? Eh?"

Pip shook his head.

"A short-tailed shrew is about our size," The Gapper explained, "and his coat is charcoal grey. He has a stubby body, a bobbed tail, small pink feet, a pointed nose, and little beady eyes. He preys on voles and mice, among other things. He's slow on his feet, and he's nearly as blind as a bat, but his hearing is remarkable, and his nose is as good as a fox's. He has twenty-two razor-sharp, red-tipped teeth. If he bites you, you will die from the poison in his saliva. Chark's a nasty customer, a very nasty customer indeed!

"He hunts around the clock, day and night," The Gapper

added, hardly drawing a breath. "And his favourite path is along the bank of this stream. Here, take a sniff of this leaf. You can smell his musk. He's been along here recently—very recently. Now I simply must go. I have things to do, important things. Like getting a drink. We voles often drink ten times a day. It was nice meeting you, young fellow, very nice indeed!"

The Gapper bustled off, his chestnut stripe barely visible in the growing darkness. "There's lots of owls around, so watch out for them, too!" he warned.

Alone and worried that Chark might appear at any moment, Pip decided to leave the stream. Just then he heard a soft *hoo, hoo, hoo* from the woods. The sound made his blood run cold, and he drummed his paws nervously. Should he stay or should he go? If he stayed, he might be caught by Chark. But if he left, an owl might get him.

Pip chose to go.

Cautiously he worked his way into the woods. Whenever he came to an open patch, he stopped first to check for danger, then scurried across the clearing as fast as his legs would carry him. He didn't see anything, although a number of times he heard other small creatures rustling in the undergrowth.

Eventually he emerged from the woods into an overgrown field that reminded him of the Prairies. Sitting on a leaf with his tail curled around him, he gazed at the stars and felt dreadfully homesick.

Then the distant hoot of an owl reminded him that he must find shelter before dawn.

Pip spotted a hedge that enclosed the remains of a split-rail fence running from the edge of the trees through the field. Halfway along the hedge was an elm tree that had lost several limbs, and one of them, as thick as a baseball bat, was buried in the grass. After sniffing to make sure nobody else lived there, Pip wormed his way under the fallen branch.

He discovered it would make an excellent den. He cleared a nest for himself and then crept outside to explore the field. A field was familiar territory, and he set off with confidence.

Soon he came face to face with another male deer mouse. Pip had no idea it was Pero, the leader of the mouse community.

The two mice stopped in their tracks. Then they edged closer, their bodies stretched forward. Pero, who was much bigger, glared at Pip with whiskers bristling and ears erect. Pip didn't want to fight, so he closed his eyes and folded back his ears.

"What are you doing here?" Pero demanded rudely.

"I … I … I came here on a train," Pip stammered.

"I'm the boss here. You're not welcome in my territory."

"But I don't have anywhere else to go!"

Pero scowled. "You can stay here for now," he said grudgingly, "but don't get in my way. And don't bother any of the local mice."

With a haughty flick of his tail, Pero stalked across the field. Pip was so disheartened that he went straight back to his den. Lying hidden at the entrance, he concluded sadly that this new place, where he had hoped to make a home, was dangerous and unfriendly. Once again he was overcome by a wave of homesickness.

An hour or so before dawn Pip heard the dainty patter of a mouse approaching. His sensitive ears told him it was a deer mouse, but the rhythm of its steps was strange. Staying absolutely still, not daring to twitch a whisker, he waited. Then he saw her ... a delicate young female with a white star on her forehead. As she came closer, he noticed she walked with a limp.

"Hi!" Pip blurted out.

The little mouse froze at the sound of his voice.

"I'm sorry! I didn't mean to scare you! My name's Pip, what's yours?"

The little mouse regained her composure, looked Pip in the eye, and said quietly, "My name's Meg."

And then she vanished.

FOUR

A New Friend

During the next few weeks Pip made nightly forays to learn the terrain. He discovered that his home was bordered by fields scattered with hawthorn bushes, alder thickets, and poplar stands. Shimmering in the distance was a small lake rimmed with cottages.

Pip often daydreamed about Meg. He was enchanted by her mysterious manner. Many times he caught a fleeting glimpse of her but nothing more. She seemed as elusive as a firefly.

He also kept an eye out for Pero, the head mouse. Pip didn't want to run into him again. Twice he spied Pero in the distance, and both times he made detours to stay out of his way.

One night, while he was scurrying across a clearing among the alders, Pip nearly collided with another mouse. Both squeaked in fright and stopped in midstride.

The other mouse was Meg.

Acadia the Saw-whet Owl witnessed this little drama from her perch atop a cedar tree. She was most intrigued. Hardly bigger than a robin, she loved to eat mice. Turning her round head first one way and then the other, she used her ears to pinpoint the exact location of the squeaks. Silently she left her perch and floated down to seize her prey.

Pip and Meg were about to touch noses when they saw her shadow. They leaped apart and fled. An instant later Acadia's talons raked the spot where Pip and Meg had been. Having missed her chance, Acadia flew to another tree, clicking her beak in frustration.

Pip and Meg both raced for a rotted stump beside a hawbush. Pip scurried in among the roots, while Meg ran in from the other side.

"Is that you, Meg?" Pip panted.

"Yes. That was close!"

Together, they retreated into the depths of the stump.

"It won't be safe to go out for some time," said Pip, "but that's okay, we can get to know each other."

Pip told Meg about the loss of his family, the encounter with Tombo, and the train ride east. Meg listened closely, squeaking with surprise and sympathy.

"So you see, Meg," Pip said, "I'm an outsider. According to Pero, you shouldn't have anything to do with me."

"Don't be so sure, Pip...."

Meg had been born that spring in a fluffy nest hollowed out of a mattress at one of the cottages on the lake. She was the smallest in her litter but the most agile of the three babies. As soon as their eyes opened, she and her two brothers played together happily.

Their carefree life ended when the humans who owned the cottage came for the summer. Mr. and Mrs. Benson and their two children, Peter and Sarah, also brought Oscar, the family cat. From the moment they arrived, the cottage was strewn with mousetraps and patrolled by Oscar. Danger lurked everywhere, so the mouse family moved out of the cottage into a nook under the porch. Meg's mother warned her children to stay near the nest. Under no circumstances were they to venture inside the cottage.

But Meg's brothers didn't listen. Early one morning they made a daring sortie into the kitchen and stuffed themselves with bread. Brimming with confidence, they raided the kitchen again the

next night. One of the mice, following a scent of cheese, blundered into a mousetrap. Oscar, alerted by the *snap!,* bounded into the kitchen and pounced on the other hapless mouse. In the space of a minute Meg lost both her brothers.

Fearing for their own lives, Meg and her mother stayed close to their den for the best part of a week, foraging on what little food they could find in the bare space under the cottage—a spider, a beetle or two, a few caterpillars. Knowing they would starve on this meagre fare, Meg's mother decided they would have to leave the den.

"We'll have to go to the lake for food." She sighed. "I know Oscar will be on the prowl, Meg, but it's a risk we'll have to take."

That night, when all was quiet, the two mice stole across the moonlit lawn and disappeared into the shrubbery by the lake. They meandered along the shoreline, picking up grubs and pulling down grass seeds and lapping water. At dawn they tiptoed back to the cottage, leaving a trail of tiny footprints in the dew.

Oscar, crouched behind a peony bush, was waiting for them. Meg and her mother had almost reached the cottage when the cat sprang from his hiding place. Meg's mother escaped by jumping to one side and scooting under the porch. Meg panicked and ran across the lawn. Oscar raced after her, stabbed out a paw, and pinned her to the ground. When she tried to wiggle free, he unsheathed his needle-sharp claws.

Then, to Meg's astonishment, the cat released her. Meg took a few cautious steps and began to run. But just when she thought she was free, Oscar stopped her with a flick of his paw. Over and over again he let her go. Over and over again he swiped her with his claws. Each time he caught her, Oscar drew blood as he raked her back. Exhausted, and weakened by the loss of blood, Meg crumpled into a tiny heap. The cat, seeing that the game was over, picked her up in his mouth. As he tightened his grip, he punctured

the muscle of her thigh with one of his fangs. Meg fainted from the pain.

At that moment Peter and Sarah came out onto the porch to watch the sun rise. When Oscar saw the children, he pranced towards them with an affectionate *meeeoww* and dropped his trophy at their feet. The children stared at the bedraggled little bundle of fur.

"Oscar caught another mouse," Peter said, cupping Meg in his hands. "Poor thing, I think it's dead."

"Let me see," said Sarah, taking the limp form from her brother. "No, it's still breathing. It's alive!"

Carrying Meg gently, Sarah tiptoed into her parents' bedroom. Mr. Benson was about to order her to take the mouse outside, but then he noticed the look of distress on his daughter's face. "Bring it over here," he said, "and I'll see if there's anything we can do."

Mr. Benson put on his glasses, switched on the bedside lamp, and carefully examined Meg. "It's a young female deer mouse. She's got some nasty scratches on her back and a bite in her thigh.

If we put some disinfectant on the wounds and keep her quiet, there's a chance she'll survive. But I can't promise."

"Where should we put her, Dad?" asked Peter.

"Why don't you use the old birdcage that's in the back room. If you roll up some loose toilet paper and put it in the bottom, she can make a nest. Oh, and cover the cage with a dish towel. It will make her feel more secure."

"What are we going to we feed her?"

"She won't be hungry for a while, but she'll be thirsty. Put water in a saucer, and mix in some honey or corn syrup. That will help her regain her strength."

When Meg awoke, her throat was dry and she ached all over. Painfully she dragged herself over to the saucer and drank a few drops. Sarah, whose face was pressed against the bars of the cage, gasped when she saw Meg stir.

"Peter! Come here. The mouse is awake. She's going to be all right!"

Strangely, Meg wasn't frightened by the humans. She sensed they meant her no harm, and she didn't mind being watched by two pairs of large blue eyes.

The next day Meg nibbled on an oatmeal cookie that Sarah gave her, and within a week she was almost better, except for her leg. Meg would always walk with a limp, but she could still run and even climb the bars of her cage.

When Mr. Benson saw her flit along the narrow perch bar and jump lightly to the floor, he knew it was time to set her free. "Sarah," he said, "your patient is ready to be discharged from hospital."

"But, Dad, can't we keep her? She's so sweet. If we let her go, Oscar will catch her again!"

"She's a wild creature, dear. Her home is the outdoors. But

30

you're absolutely right about Oscar. What we'll do is set her free in the field on the far side of the lake."

That evening Mr. Benson drove Sarah and Peter to the field. When they got there, Sarah set the cage down and opened the door. For a moment Meg wouldn't move. Then she limped to the door and jumped out. As she disappeared into the grass, Sarah, with tears in her eyes, called after her, "Goodbye, little mouse."

At first Meg was frightened and lonely, but after a few weeks she settled into her new surroundings and even made some new friends, including The Gapper. The local deer mice were polite but treated her like a stranger.

Pero was especially unkind. "You won't make any mouse friends around here, and don't expect to," he sneered.

"But ... why not?" Meg asked, bewildered.

"Because you're different. You walk funny."

Meg didn't respond. She resolved then and there to make her own way—with or without the help of the mouse community.

"So you see, Pip, we're both outsiders," Meg said, snuggling up against him.

"Oh, Meg," Pip replied. "Now we can be friends!"

FIVE

STRANGE ENCOUNTERS

As soon as it was safe to leave the stump, Pip and Meg scampered home—down through the alders, across the field, and along the hedge. Pip's new friend, Meg, it turned out, was also his neighbour!

He had often passed her den, but it was so cleverly hidden that he hadn't noticed it. Meg showed him how she had arranged the grass so no one could tell she lived there. With this lesson in mind, Pip took a hard look at his own home. He realized that from certain angles it was easy to spot the entrance. It was so obvious that he was lucky he hadn't been discovered by one of his many enemies.

To hide it, he cut a sheaf of grass with his sharp front teeth and carried the bundle in his mouth to the entrance. Then, using his paws, he carefully arranged the grass, as Meg had done, to camouflage it. Next, he gnawed another opening at the back of his den. This gave him an emergency exit, and because it was hidden by the foliage, he could come and go in secret.

Like most deer mice, Pip had other homes that he used if he was caught away from his main den when the sun came up. The simplest was a roll of grass in the meadow, the most elaborate a robin's nest in a gnarled apple tree.

The nest was Pip's favourite. The scaly bark on the tree made it easy to climb, and he liked padding along the limb to the empty nest. The location was ideal—high enough to be out of the way of his largest enemies, but low enough for him to reach easily.

Pip converted the nest to his own use. He kicked the old debris over the side with his hind feet and carefully lined the nest with fresh grass, patting it into place with his paws. Then he made a roof by laying twigs across the rim in a crisscross pattern. Over the twigs he spread grass to keep out the sun and the rain. Around the rim, he left openings for an entrance and several spy holes. As a final touch, he placed three dead leaves on top for camouflage. From a distance the den looked exactly like an abandoned bird's nest.

Pip could hardly wait to show Meg his tree house. By coincidence, he met her on his way home. "Meg," he cried, "come with me. I've got something to show you!"

Pip was so enthusiastic that she couldn't resist the invitation. But when he started to climb the apple tree, she was totally mystified. Bursting with curiosity, she followed him up the trunk and out onto the limb.

"What do you think?" he asked proudly, pointing to the nest. Meg made a great show of studying it, stepping forward and backwards, looking at the nest from all angles. Pip drummed his paws, waiting anxiously for her verdict.

"It's perfect," she said finally. "Let's go inside."

Pip often spent the daylight hours in the apple tree. Waking from a doze, he would peep out one of the spy holes, and sometimes, as he sleepily rested his chin on the rim, he let his tail dangle out a hole on the other side.

One evening Pip was dreamily gazing at the world when he spied something unusual on the ground. It was another mouse. But a most peculiar one. It had pale-yellow fur on its sides, long spindly legs, and a very long tail. As Pip watched, the mouse suddenly made a tremendous leap right over a tall milkweed

plant. Pip was astonished. This mouse could jump like a grasshopper!

The mouse stopped near the tree to eat some grass seeds, and Pip quietly slipped to the ground. When the mouse saw Pip, he leaped high in the air. As soon as he landed, he made another bound, and then stopped in his tracks. Slowly Pip crept towards the stranger until they were almost touching.

"What sort of mouse are you?" asked Pip.

"I'm a meadow-jumping mouse," said Zap, the visitor, as he flexed a long, skinny hind leg. "Jumping's my name and jumping's my game!" Zap made one of his prodigious leaps and, looking immensely pleased with himself, returned in a single bound. Pip was impressed—and envious.

"I wish I could jump like that," he said. "We deer mice have an escape leap, but it's not half as good as yours."

"Of course it isn't. We're the champion jumpers of the mouse world."

"Does that mean that you never have to worry about enemies?"

"Not exactly, but nobody can catch me when I'm in the air. Chark the Short-tailed Shrew tried to corner me the other night, and I just flew over his head." He chuckled. "Chark still doesn't know where I went!

"I do have to watch out, though. When I'm eating or snoozing, I sometimes get careless. Last week I was dozing in the meadow, and I nearly got eaten by a big snake. The thing about snakes is they're so quiet."

Zap finished his meal and then headed off across the meadow. Pip, hoping to see him pop above the grass, watched until his new friend disappeared into the gloom.

Pip thought about Zap as he made his way to the edge of the forest. He was so preoccupied that he strayed deeper and deeper into the woods. The eerie call of an owl, *hoo, hoo, hoo,* jolted him out of his reverie. Realizing the owl was nearby, he retraced his steps and hurried back to the field. He was halfway across the last clearing when danger struck.

An owl swooped out of the darkness like a thunderbolt. It came so close that Pip felt the wind from its wings. Strangely, it didn't touch him. Looking up, Pip saw it was heading for him again. At the last moment the owl banked sharply and struck a large white moth. It was then that Pip realized it wasn't an owl at all—but a harmless hoary bat!

By now it was late August. The days were still warm, but the nights were cool, and the sky was often lit by the Northern Lights. Pip sometimes stopped to marvel at the rays of green and purple dancing across the heavens.

August also brought lots of wild berries. Pip especially liked blueberries and would venture a long way to feast on them. One night he stayed out so long that when he set off for home, it was nearly dawn. Rather than make the long trek to his den in the hedge, he decided to spend the day in his nearest hideaway, the roll of grass at the edge of the meadow. When he finally reached it, he fell asleep instantly.

The morning sun burned the dew off the grass, and by noon it was as warm as a midsummer day. Lulled by the heat, Pip slept soundly, waking only briefly to check for enemies. It was mid-afternoon when his sixth sense alerted him. Something was wrong. Drowsily he looked outside at the grass swaying in the breeze but saw nothing. He was about to drop off to sleep again when the breeze brought him a faint musty scent.

Pip was instantly awake. It might be Chark, but the shrew probably wouldn't be working the open meadow. It might also be a skunk, but skunks rarely travel in daylight. Anxiously Pip sniffed the breeze to identify the sinister scent. The smell grew stronger. He knew what it was—a snake!

Pip cautiously peered outside. This time he examined every blade of grass, but try as he might, he could see no sign of this dreaded foe. When he was about to flee from his refuge, he heard a rustle directly in front of the entrance and saw the mottled length of a huge garter snake slide by. The snake stopped and turned. Very slowly a great smooth head rose before Pip.

Hypnotized by its glittering black eyes, Pip couldn't move a muscle. The head came closer, a blood-red tongue forking in and out from the slit of its mouth. His heart pounding as though it would burst, Pip waited for the end. The snake edged forward. Pip saw its mouth open wide and the glint of fangs.

Suddenly the sun was blotted out, and there was a thunderous clapping of wings. Pip's fragile refuge shook violently. Although it seemed like ages, the commotion lasted only seconds. Then there was silence. Looking up in stunned disbelief, Pip saw a red-shouldered hawk fly away with the snake writhing in its grip.

Pip had been saved by one of his enemies!

SIX

AUTUMN

It was October, the time of scarlet and gold. The scented air was crisp, and for a few nights the countryside was flooded with light by a giant harvest moon. Autumn had arrived, and Pip knew he must prepare for winter.

By September he had reached his full size and put on a lot of weight. He wasn't chubby, but he had a layer of fat that would help keep him warm when the snow came. He had also lost his baby fur. His adult coat, buff above and white below, was thick and glossy.

One morning the grass was covered with frost, and there were cobwebs of ice on the puddles. Pip's den was so cold that he could see his breath. Shivering, he drummed his paws on the frozen ground and wondered what to do. Then it came to him. The best way to stay warm would be to live in an underground den. Pip knew a perfect place, and it wasn't far away, just along the hedge. He would investigate it that very night.

The spot he had in mind was beneath an old stump. An abandoned den of Stripey the Chipmunk, it had a funnel-shaped entrance among the roots that went straight down, then narrowed into a long, winding tunnel with short passages branching off to the sides. Pip followed the main tunnel and eventually came to Stripey's old sleeping chamber. The oval-shaped room had a musty smell and was filled with shredded leaves. Pip didn't like being so far underground, so he retraced his steps and decided to make his den in a passage closer to the entrance.

Digging with his paws and pushing the dirt out of the way with his hind legs, he cleared the plug of leaves that Stripey had used to block the passage. When Pip punched through to the surface, he saw that he had discovered a hidden exit! Then he carved out his winter home. He worked furiously, even though his eyes smarted from the dust and his coat got clogged with earth. It was hard going, but after a few hours he had a cozy room to sleep in. Tomorrow night he would come back and line it with thistledown.

Pip was so proud of himself that he climbed onto the stump and sang for joy. Humans couldn't hear his trills because his voice was too high, but many of the forest creatures heard his song.

One of them was Pero, the leader of the mouse community. Pero listened for a minute, then angrily headed for the stump to teach this saucy intruder a lesson.

"You up there," Pero cried, "stop that racket at once!"

"I'm only singing because I'm happy," Pip replied. "I've nearly finished making my winter den."

"Well, you can't live there. This is my territory. Now get out!"

Pip was not going to let himself be bullied. Nor was he going to leave his new home.

"I'm not bothering you, Pero, and I have every right to live here."

Enraged by Pip's defiance, Pero jumped onto the stump and stared at the young mouse. Baring his teeth, Pero squealed, "Move—or else!"

Pip was terrified, but he stood his ground. A second later Pero charged at him. At first Pip was able to block the blows with his paws, but then Pero grabbed him in a stranglehold. Locked together like wrestlers, they rolled back and forth biting and scratching.

Pip had long dreaded this showdown. But to his amazement, he was holding his own—and even getting in a few good licks. As the fight continued, the two mice rolled closer and closer to the edge

of the stump. The next thing Pip knew, they were falling through space.

Smack! They hit the ground with such force they flew apart. Moments later they were on their feet. Glaring, Pero ran at Pip. Then, all of a sudden, Pero stopped, turned, and walked away.

"I've got better things to do than waste my time with you," Pero muttered.

Panting from exhaustion, Pip took a long time to catch his breath. Slowly he clambered back up the stump. Then it dawned on him. He had defied Pero, and Pero had been the first to back down. From now on, Pip could go where he pleased without having to worry about that big bully. Pip was so happy that he raised his nose to the sky and began to sing again.

Meg, on her way home, heard Pip and hurried over. She was horrified to see her friend covered with dirt and streaked with blood. "What in the world happened to you, Pip?"

Pip was barely able to contain himself. "Pero tried to bully me, but I stood up to him."

"Oh, Pip! I'm so proud of you I feel like singing, too!"

Meg hopped onto the stump. Sitting side by side, the two little outcasts happily serenaded the moon.

The next night Pip carefully climbed a field thistle to collect some down for his den. It was a tricky job—the prickly spines kept getting in his way. While he was aloft, he spotted Zap the Meadow-jumping Mouse and squeaked a greeting. Zap was fat now and moved as though he were half asleep.

"What's the matter, Zap?"

"Nothing, Pip. I'm about to hibernate, that's all."

"'Hibernate'? What does that mean?"

"It means that one of these days I'm going to plug the entrance to my den, curl up in my chamber, and sleep until next spring. That's why I've put on so much weight—my fat will keep me warm and feed me while I'm asleep."

"Gosh! Hibernating seems like an odd thing to do!"

"It's not odd for a meadow-jumping mouse, or for a skunk or a woodchuck, for that matter. We always do, it's our nature." He paused to yawn. "Take care of yourself, Pip. See you next spring."

As Zap lazily wandered off, Pip went back to gathering thistledown. When he had filled his mouth with silky fibres, he climbed down and carried them back to the stump. After he spread the floss, he realized it would take a good many trips to cover the floor of his den. To save time on the next trip, he took a shortcut through the alders.

He was in the middle of a thicket when two owls flew towards him. There was nowhere to hide—the ground was bare beneath the alders—and there was no time to run. In desperation, Pip scuttled under a fallen leaf. To his horror both owls fluttered down beside him. One was almost close enough to touch. Hardly daring to breathe, Pip peeped out from under the leaf.

They weren't owls, but birds he'd never seen before!

They had long bills, plump round bodies, and coats that were a delicate patchwork of russet-brown feathers. As he watched, one of them rose on his stick legs and probed the moist soil with his bill. The bird was drilling for something, his bill sinking deeper and deeper into the earth. Pip was fascinated.

"What are you doing?" he asked the nearest bird.

The bird jerked his bill out of the ground and studied Pip with large black eyes.

"You startled me! You deer mice are all the same, always creeping around, afraid of your own shadow.

"But to answer your question," he said in a kinder tone, "I'm boring for worms. I'm Rusty the Woodcock. That's my sister Tess over there. The ground's frozen up north, and we haven't eaten since yesterday."

While the two woodcock punched holes in the earth, Pip saw several others flit into the alders.

"How long do you plan to stay?" Pip asked Rusty.

"I've no idea. We're on our way south. We could stay a few hours, a few days, or even a few weeks. A lot depends on the weather. We like to travel when the moon is full, but if there's a cold snap, we'll ride the North Wind."

"Will I see you again?"

"Well, you might, and then again you might not. We're unpredictable, you know!"

High above, Pip heard the sound of Canada geese. Tuning his ears to their wild cries, he sat on his haunches and scanned the sky.

42

Presently he caught sight of the majestic birds silhouetted against the moon. Like Rusty and Tess, the geese were heading south.

The next morning Pip was wakened by the honking of another wedge of geese, passing directly overhead. Blinking in the sun, he watched them until they were specks on the horizon. As he turned to go back to his den, there was a twitter of wings, and Rusty glided into the hedge.

"What are you doing here, Rusty?" Pip asked. "It's not a good place to find worms—there's too many rocks."

"I'm not looking for worms. All I want is a quiet place to nap."

Wiggling his short tail to get comfortable, Rusty hunkered down with his head on his breast and fell asleep. Pip rubbed his eyes and looked again. Rusty's feathers blended so perfectly with the autumn leaves that he was almost invisible!

The tinkle of a distant bell woke Pip around noon. The sound faded and then grew stronger. Puzzled, he climbed onto the stump to get a better look. Running along the hedge was a white and brown dog with a bell around its neck. Behind the dog was a man wearing a red hat and carrying a gun.

"Wake up, Rusty! There's a human coming with a dog!"

Rusty, now wide awake, didn't seem concerned.

"Don't worry, Pip, I've been through this before. Just watch!"

When the dog was opposite the stump, it stopped like a statue. Scenting the breeze, it slowly turned its head and pointed its nose at the spot where Rusty was crouched. Expecting the woodcock to flush, the man walked past the dog. But Rusty didn't move. Exasperated, the man walked into the brushy hedge and passed right by his quarry. As soon as the man's back was turned, Rusty sprang into the air and darted away in the opposite direction. By the time the hunter realized what had happened, the woodcock was gone.

That night Pip visited the alders and found Rusty and Tess still there.

"That was a lucky escape this afternoon, Rusty," Pip said.

"It wasn't luck, Pip, it was a trick I often use. When you're in a tight corner, the best way to escape is to surprise your enemy." Rusty looked Pip in the eye. "Remember that, it could save your life."

The next day the temperature dropped, and a brisk north wind stripped most of the colour from the trees. When Pip returned to the alder patch that night, he found it deserted. Rusty and Tess had gone south.

SEVEN

Two Close Calls

By now the forest was carpeted with leaves, and the fields looked as though they had been swept by a broom. The autumn sun had lost its warmth, and the days were growing shorter. During the long frosty nights Pip spent much of his time gathering food.

His den was already well stocked for winter. Clover seeds, dandelion seeds, apple seeds, and cherry pits were all carefully heaped in piles. In his storeroom, which he had dug a little way along the tunnel, there were acorns and beechnuts, mushrooms and red hawberries. Outside his den, he had buried smaller caches of food.

Other woodland creatures were also hoarding food. It was a busy time for all the animals, especially the squirrels, who had harvested the acorns under the big oak tree.

Passing under the oak tree one evening, Pip found a fresh acorn. He was delighted by this windfall and decided to have it for supper. Sitting on his haunches, he rotated the nut with his paws and gnawed a hole in the pointed end. Then, to get at the meat inside, he gripped the acorn firmly in his paws and tore the shell open with his front teeth.

Nearby was a tall milkweed plant bursting with seeds. As Pip climbed the stalk, he brushed against a pod, releasing a shower of seeds that drifted off in the breeze like tiny parachutes. Near the top he came upon a canoe-shaped pod packed as tightly as corn

46

on a cob. Pip steadied the pod with his paws and used his teeth to separate the flat brown seeds from their silvery tails.

While Pip was filling his cheeks with seeds, he noticed a tunnel in the grass—a hidden pathway used by red-backed voles. Soon a vole came into view, and for a moment Pip thought it was The Gapper. But it wasn't. It was a young vole that meandered along, stopping now and then to sniff the grass. The vole disappeared around a bend, and another creature came shuffling along the trail, his pointed nose close to the ground. Dark-grey coat, chunky body, short tail, and mean little eyes. There was no mistaking him—it was Chark the Short-tailed Shrew!

Pip was in a terrible predicament. He wanted to sound an alarm, but he knew the slightest noise would give him away. There was nothing he could do. To his horror he saw the young vole reappear around the bend and head straight for Chark. Scenting his prey, Chark became excited and broke into a trot. Pip, forgetting his own safety, squeaked a warning. The vole looked up and saw the shrew, but it was too late. With a squeal of triumph, Chark charged at the vole and bit him on the shoulder. They struggled briefly, and then the vole tore free and started running down the path.

After a few steps the vole began to pant and stagger as the poison from the shrew's saliva did its work. His strength fading, the vole wobbled to a stop and collapsed. Chark confidently approached his victim. He gloated over the helpless vole for a moment before sinking his pointed teeth into the vole's neck. With horrible crunching noises, Chark ate the vole.

Pip witnessed the entire incident and felt ill. Vowing to avoid Chark forever, he quietly slid down his perch and raced home.

A few nights later Pip saw another red-backed vole in the distance. When it came closer, he noticed something familiar about its bustling gait.

"I'm so glad to see you, Mr. Gapper. I've been worrying about you!" Breathlessly Pip told his friend about Chark and the young vole.

"That vole was one of my nephews, one of my many nephews," The Gapper said sadly. "The young are often careless, and you can't afford to be careless with Chark. A dreadful end, truly dreadful!"

"Have you had any close calls with Chark?"

"No. I keep my wits about me, and so should you, Pip. Not only with Chark, but now that winter's coming, you're going to have to watch out for Stoaty the Ermine and his mate, Mustella."

"I've heard about Stoaty and Mustella, and I've often smelled their musky scent, but I've never actually seen them."

"Stoaty's as big as a red squirrel, and Mustella is half his size. They have long thin bodies, short legs, pointy heads, and little round ears. During the summer their coat is dark brown above and white below. But when winter arrives, their coats turn pure white, except for the black tip of their tails."

The Gapper paused. "They like to hunt in pairs, and they move very fast. They're busiest at dawn and at dusk, and they especially like to eat mice."

While Pip was digesting this unpleasant information, The Gapper excused himself and headed purposefully for the stream. "I must get a drink, a drink," he muttered.

On his way home Pip saw Meg, sitting outside her den in the moonlight. She was drumming her paws on the ground.

"What's on your mind, Meg?"

"I'd like to visit the cottage where I was born and see my mother," Meg replied.

"But wouldn't that be dangerous, with the cat and the humans?"

"It could be dangerous, I suppose. But the humans have left for the winter."

Meg absent-mindedly began to drum her paws again. In the moonlight Pip could see the white star on her forehead. Finally Meg made up her mind. "I think I'll go," she said. "Would you like to come?"

Pip, torn between caution and curiosity, hesitated a moment but decided to go.

At dusk the next day the two mice set off. They scurried along the hedge, under the fence, and across the lower field to the edge of the lake. There, they followed the shoreline to the cottages. The journey took several hours.

All the cottages were deserted, except for one. Meg's old home had a station wagon in the driveway. The Bensons had chosen this weekend to close their cottage for the winter.

Dismayed, Meg turned to Pip. "I'm so sorry. I didn't know the humans would be here."

"Well, Meg, we can still visit your mother. We don't have to go inside."

"You're right, but first we must check to see if the cat's outside."

Cautiously Meg and Pip tiptoed around the cottage, stopping frequently to sniff the wind and to listen. There was no sign of Oscar. Satisfied that it was safe, they crept under the porch to visit Meg's mother. Her den was filled with cobwebs and hadn't been used for weeks.

Meg's heart sank.

"What's happened to Mother?" she squeaked.

"Don't worry, Meg. I'm sure she's just moved to a safer place. Look, the best thing for us to do now is to have a rest and then start back."

Sadly Meg cleaned out the den so that she and Pip could curl up for a nap. Pip had barely fallen asleep when Meg nudged him awake. "Would you like to see inside the cottage?" she asked mischievously. "I've been listening. The humans have gone to bed, and I'm sure it's safe."

"I guess so," Pip said reluctantly. "But only for a minute."

Meg led the way. Hopping onto one of the posts, she ran along a supporting beam and climbed through a crack in the kitchen floor. After Pip squeezed through the opening, he stood on his hind legs and looked around the room. It was very strange.

"I've seen enough, Meg. Let's go back."

"There's nothing to worry about, Pip. Oscar's not around, and there might be some food."

Meg picked up a familiar sweet scent. Sure enough, in a corner of the kitchen Meg found a large oatmeal cookie just like the one Sarah had fed her when she was hurt. The cookie was on a little plate inside a wire box that was open at one end. Meg crept into the cage and started to nibble at the cookie. Pip watched for a moment, then followed her inside.

Clang! The end of the box snapped shut.

Pip and Meg frantically searched for a way out, but it was no use. They were trapped!

Fortunately Sarah was the first human to come into the kitchen the next morning. When she saw the trap had been sprung, she went over to the box and looked inside. Her eyes widened with disbelief.

"Peter! Come and see what we've caught!"

Fascinated, the two children stared at the mice.

"See the little one in the corner with the white mark on her forehead," Sarah said. "I'm sure she's the one we saved from Oscar. She's come back!"

By this time Mr. Benson had come into the kitchen. Sarah was bubbling with excitement at seeing her little pet again.

"Dad, what about the other mouse? Do you think it's her mate?"

"I really don't know, dear. But it's bigger than she is, so it's probably a male. It could be her mate—or her brother."

After breakfast Mr. Benson put the trap in the station wagon and drove with the children to the other side of the lake. At the

edge of the field Sarah opened the door of the trap, and the mice scampered into the grass.

"Good luck!" she cried.

Exhausted by their ordeal, Meg and Pip didn't go very far. As they were making their way along a drainage ditch, they came upon an abandoned mouse nest.

"Let's stay here until sundown," said Meg. "It'll be safer after dark."

Curling up inside the ragged ball of grass, Pip and Meg slept fitfully for the rest of the day. When they set off again, the sun was a red glow on the horizon.

Meg was limping noticeably, and both she and Pip were extremely nervous. Crossing the field, they jumped at every little sound. But nothing happened—until they reached the hedge.

There, Pip and Meg caught the faint scent of a red fox, one of their dreaded enemies. The two mice crouched motionless, sniffing the breeze. Then they took a few steps forward and checked again. The odour was stronger. The fox was ahead of them.

Treading quietly, their nerves on edge, Pip and Meg pressed on. Halfway along the hedge, they realized the fox had veered off across the meadow. They were nearly home now, and the way ahead was clear. With relief, they paused to catch their breath under a tall maple tree.

Suddenly they heard movement above them. Pip and Meg bolted into the hedge seconds before a crimson maple leaf floated to the ground.

"Meg, it's only a leaf!"

They both looked up. The tree was bare. It was the last leaf of autumn.

EIGHT

The First Snow

It got much colder in November. One night the sky became overcast, and a mysterious silence settled over the field. When Pip went to bed just before dawn, he felt restless and couldn't get to sleep. He fussed and fidgeted for hours. Puzzled by the unusual hush, he padded out of his den and climbed onto the stump to see what was happening.

As if by magic, the countryside had been transformed from brown to white. The grass, the bushes, even the branches of the trees were covered with a mantle of snow. A few lazy flakes still drifted from the sky, and Pip caught one on his tongue. He felt an icy pinprick, and then it melted. Sticking out his tongue again, he tried to catch another, but this time the flake landed in his eye. It smarted and made him blink.

Gingerly he crept about on top of the stump. The snow was cold but not uncomfortable. Gaining confidence, Pip clambered down and made a little tour around the stump. How easy it was to move about in the snow! Then he jumped back up and looked at his tracks—a series of four little dots forming a perfect circle.

Except for his tracks, there wasn't a sign of another living creature. This made Pip feel a little lonely. Suddenly a hoarse *jaay! jaay!* broke the stillness, and a bluejay flew along the hedge. With a *whirr* of wings the brilliantly coloured bird lit on a rosebush, dislodging a shower of snow. Raising its crest, it happily whistled, *Too-wheedle, too-wheedle,* and began to gobble a frosty rosehip. The jay's good humour made Pip feel better. Maybe winter wouldn't be so bad after all.

That night, when Pip set off on his rounds, the sky was clear. Snow crystals glittered in the moonlight. Crossing the field, Pip paused to savour the enchanting scene. Then he spied The Gapper carefully making his way along the edge of the woods. Pip hurried over to see his friend.

"Hi, Mr. Gapper! Isn't the snow wonderful?"

"Well, hello there, Pip! Hello! Yes indeed, yes indeed, but there isn't enough snow."

"What do you mean?"

"Right now the snow is only a few inches deep, and we have to travel on top of it. That's very dangerous, very dangerous. You spotted me across the field. That means our enemies can see us from far away, too."

Pip thought about this for a moment. He was puzzled. "How is more snow going to help us?"

"When it gets deeper, we can dig tunnels and live under the snow. Much safer that way, much safer."

"But isn't it awfully cold under the snow?"

"Not in the least. There's no wind, and when a few of us huddle together, it's snug and warm. But best of all, when you want a drink, you just have to eat some snow. I do it all the time."

The Gapper gathered some snow in his paws and popped it into his mouth. Pip tried a mouthful and found that, as usual, The Gapper was right.

"I must go," said The Gapper. "If we stand around here much longer, an owl will get us." With that, he trundled into the woods.

Pip, now mindful of how easy it was to be seen against the snow, took extra care on his way home. As he returned across the field, a small shrub flickered in the shadows. He stopped and stared at the white mound. Then it started to move!

"Boots, I thought you were a bush!" Pip exclaimed.

"Coming from you, Pip, that's a compliment," the snowshoe hare replied, twitching his ears with amusement. "That's why my winter coat is white, to blend with the snow."

Boots raised a large hind leg and showed Pip the stiff pad of hairs on the sole of his foot. "See, I'm well equipped for winter. I've even got snowshoes!"

After Boots left, Pip continued on his way, pausing frequently to check for danger. For some reason he was very nervous. Once again he stopped and looked around. In the moonlight he could see every feature of the field. Nothing to worry about there. Slowly he turned his head and scanned the hedge. His heart skipped a beat. On the far side, sitting motionless, was Nick the Red Fox.

Nick and Pip stared at each other for a moment. Then Pip dashed for his den. Quick as a flash, the fox darted through the hedge to intercept him. But Pip leaped to one side. Running for his life, he zigzagged through the brushy hedge. With a series of bounds that sent the snow flying, Nick followed Pip's every move.

Pip had almost reached safety when Nick pounced and pinned him to the snow. Squirming desperately, Pip managed to wriggle free. Nick's teeth snapped shut a hair's breadth away. Panic-stricken, Pip ran under the fox, and then changed direction. For a few seconds the fox didn't know where Pip had gone. By the time Nick realized what had happened, Pip had scuttled into the stump.

Pip huddled in the tunnel below the entrance to his den. Outside, he heard the faint crunch of snow as his enemy circled the stump. Then Nick began to dig furiously and even managed to force his nose into the entrance. Pip felt the fox's hot breath and saw his glistening black muzzle. Terrified, Pip fled down the tunnel to his chamber. Eventually the scratching sounds stopped.

The fox, defeated by the tangle of roots, had given up. A little while later, Pip heard Nick's steps receding in the distance.

Pip was so frightened that he didn't leave his home until the next morning, and even then it was only to inspect the damage. Nick had made quite a mess, but the thick roots protecting the entrance were still intact. His home secure, Pip went inside and dozed for the rest of the day.

That night the sight of the moon—and memories of Nick— made Pip so uncomfortable that he decided to stay inside. He was just about to start eating some of his hoarded rations when he heard a small voice.

"Pip, are you in there? Are you there, Pip?"

Delighted, Pip hurried to the entrance to greet Meg.

"Oh, you're safe!" she cried. "I saw your tracks and Nick's, and I saw where he'd been digging, and I thought ..." She let the words trail off.

"I'm okay, Meg. But it's so dangerous with the snow that I don't think I want to go outside any more."

"Pip, you have to go outside. You haven't got enough food to last the winter."

Pip knew she was right, but he still didn't relish the thought.

"Why don't we go together?" Meg suggested. "Two heads are better than one, so it'll be safer—and we can keep each other company."

"That's a great idea," Pip said.

Side by side, the two mice set off to the far edge of the field. Each time they came to a bit of cover, they paused, and each time they came to an open patch, they scurried across as if chased by the devil. They didn't meet any enemies, and the trip was uneventful. On the way home Pip turned to Meg and said, "Thanks to you, I'm not scared any more!"

By Christmas the countryside was blanketed with snow. The layer between the crust and the frozen earth was riddled with tunnels made by moles, voles, and mice. Within this maze of passages were dens, storerooms, wasterooms, and large chambers where animals could huddle together. Pip's field was like an underground village.

Some of the little creatures, especially the moles, spent most of the winter under the snow. The deer mice, when it was bitterly cold, often gathered in one of the big chambers. Pip and Meg, who were still considered outsiders by the other mice, rarely huddled with them. But they used the hidden passages to travel to their favourite feeding areas.

To get to some places, though, they had to travel aboveground. They always tried to make these forays on cloudy nights so that owls wouldn't see them against the snow.

On New Year's Eve, Meg and Pip decided to have a feed of hawberries. The only bush that still held fruit was on the edge of the forest, and they would have to travel part of the way in the open. When they headed out, the moon was shrouded by thick clouds.

But just as they finished their feast, the clouds parted, and Meg and Pip found themselves bathed in moonlight.

Suddenly Meg noticed something on the far side of the field. Then it disappeared. She nudged Pip. "I think I saw Stoaty or Mustella," she whispered, pointing with her nose. "Over there."

The two mice watched the spot intently and saw a small puff of snow. From it emerged a sleek little animal with a white coat—and a black tip on its tail. Stoaty! The ermine ran along the surface for a little while and then plunged into the snow again. He was hunting for mice and voles.

There was no time to lose. If Stoaty smelled Meg and Pip, he

would chase them—even through their underground tunnels—
and most surely catch them.

As soon as a cloud covered the moon, Pip and Meg made a run
for it. Staying in the shadows, they scurried along the edge of the
forest. After a while they stopped to rest at the base of an old
poplar tree. Then, all of a sudden, something swooped out of the
darkness and landed on the tree trunk above them.

"I bet you thought I was an owl!" said a mischievous voice.

Pip and Meg looked up. Staring down at them was a big mouse
with a loose grey overcoat and a furry tail.

"Who are you?" asked Pip.

"Sabrina the Flying Squirrel."

"Can you really fly?"

"Well, I don't actually fly, but I can glide. Watch, I'll show you."

Sabrina jumped down from the tree and stretched out her
limbs, turning her coat into a cape. In a twinkling she scampered

to the top of a nearby tree. Then, with a powerful thrust of her hind legs, she launched herself into space. Using her tail to steer, she changed direction in midair and landed softly in front of Pip and Meg.

"Oh, that looks like fun!" cried Pip. "I've always wanted to fly."

Delighted to have an audience, Sabrina made many more flights. But to Pip's and Meg's dismay, drifting clouds veiled the moon, and it became too dark to see her.

The two young mice squeaked their goodbyes to Sabrina and took advantage of the darkness to make it safely home.

NINE

A Narrow Escape

The beginning of March was warm and balmy. Day after day the sun melted the snow, exposing patches of faded grass. For the first time in months Pip caught the scent of fresh earth.

But today was different. Pip sensed the weather was about to change. Sitting on his stump, he shivered as an icy gust ruffled his fur. The wind came from the northeast—a bad sign. Close-packed clouds, like skeins of dirty wool, hid the afternoon sun. Across the field a ragged string of crows flew silently to their roost.

Usually Pip wouldn't leave his den before dusk, but he knew if he waited until nightfall he might be stormbound. Was Meg thinking the same thing? Should he go now, or should he wait to see if she came by?

Rocking back and forth, he drummed the stump with his paws. His larder was bare, and if he stayed inside, he would have nothing to eat. Hunger made up his mind. He scurried down the stump and set out.

Soon the storm began—a few wet flakes at first, then a stinging wall of blinding, sifting snow. It became pitch dark, and Pip couldn't see. Alarmed, he tried to retrace his steps, but he had lost all sense of direction. Floundering through the snow sapped his strength and increased his fear. It was hopeless. Unless he found shelter soon, he would die.

Pip eventually stumbled into a cedar tree. Crawling under its green skirt, he chose a protected spot close to the trunk. Out of the wind and safe from the storm, he rolled himself into a ball and fell asleep.

He was awakened by a shaft of sunlight on his nose. Blinking at the brightness, he shook himself and stretched. Then he noticed the silence. The storm was over.

Nimbly Pip climbed to the top of the cedar tree to get his bearings. But he didn't recognize any landmarks. Anxious to find his way home, he left immediately. Progress was slow because he had to burrow through gigantic drifts and stop frequently to catch his breath. The only signs of other creatures were the tracks of a snowshoe hare and the piercing calls of a jay.

Here and there, despite the thick cloak of snow, the countryside began to look more familiar. At the top of a rise Pip paused to sniff the wind and caught the faint odour of mice. He followed the ribbon of scent to a little hillock. There, hidden at the base of a snowdrift, was a freshly dug entrance to a tunnel. With a squeak of relief, Pip ran inside.

Corridors led off in several directions, and a few whiffs told Pip which one to take. The passage curved and twisted its way into Pip's field. His excitement mounted as he crept along and the scent of mice became stronger. Soon he heard squeaks in the distance. Rounding the last bend, he came upon a domed chamber with passages branching from it like the spokes of a wheel. It was crowded with mice.

Pero, the leader, was in the centre, surrounded by other senior mice. Meg, Pip noticed, was on the fringe of the circle, with the younger mice.

When Pip entered, all conversation stopped. Pero looked at Pip with disdain.

"What are you doing here?" Pero demanded.

Pip was humiliated. "I got caught in the storm and got lost," he mumbled. "I haven't eaten since yesterday."

"Serves you right. You youngsters don't have enough brains to come in out of the rain. Or the snow." Pero chuckled. A few of the older mice laughed, too.

Pero gestured to the far side of the chamber. "You can stay for a few hours—over there. Then you must leave."

Too tired and hungry to dispute Pero's authority, Pip quietly went over and snuggled beside Meg.

"Thank goodness you're safe!" Meg whispered. "When the storm started, I went by your den and you weren't there. Then I got really worried.

"You must be starving to death! If you go down the corridor behind us, you'll find a cherry sapling that still has some bark."

Pip felt stronger after eating, and he was in better spirits when he returned.

But something was wrong. Ears erect, he strained to hear through the din of squeaks in the chamber. Then he heard it—the faint crunch of paws. He craned his neck to look at the snow ceiling. A shadow passed across the room, changing the light from milky green to grey.

"Quiet!" cried Pip, springing to his feet.

The room fell silent. Pip motioned above his head, and everyone, even Pero, turned to stare at the ceiling. Again, a fleeting shadow darkened the chamber. Then the mice heard the stealthy pad of a fox. They waited tensely, hoping they were safe in their hidden den.

Nick and his mate, Rena, made bright splashes of colour as they trotted across the sunlit field. The two foxes were hunting in tandem, weaving back and forth, tasting the breeze. On the far edge Rena caught a scent of mouse. She and Nick moved forward

65

with delicate steps, each leaving a single line of tracks in the snow. When the odour became stronger, they stopped in midstride, listening, their ears cocked towards the ground. They heard muffled squeaks through the porous crust—they had pinpointed their quarry!

The prospect of mice for supper made Nick and Rena drool with hunger. But for their hunt to be successful, they had to work as a team. If they made the slightest mistake, the mice would escape.

They knew exactly what to do. They took up positions above the mice's hideaway, Nick on his haunches, Rena across from him in a half-crouch. Their yellow eyes locked for an instant. Then, like a horse jumping a fence, Nick vaulted into the air. At the top of his arc he turned gracefully, his plume flowing behind, and plunged into the snow.

Two long black legs punched through the roof of the mice's chamber followed by a huge mouth with sharp white fangs. Pero was snatched with a crunch and flung out of the hole. Then a second set of jaws appeared, and the entire room collapsed in an avalanche of snow. Pandemonium broke loose. Another mouse was caught while trying to flee, and many more were trapped. Pip and Meg, pressed against a wall, were overlooked in the attack.

"Quick, Pip, this way!" cried Meg, running for the nearest corridor. Pip motioned to the other survivors and led the little band down the passage.

They escaped just in time. Seconds later a large snout ripped open the entrance to the tunnel. The foxes then tried to cut the mice off with a series of pounces. One was so close that part of the wall crumbled, nearly blocking the mice's way.

Scrambling through the snow, Pip and his followers turned at the next intersection and dashed along another corridor.

TEN

PIP SAVES THE DAY

"We're still in danger," Pip warned his followers. Behind them, the mice could hear Nick and Rena casting about in the snow. It was only a matter of time before the foxes found the passage and picked up the mice's scent. Ahead, there could be more danger. Ermine and short-tailed shrews patrolled the warren under the snow.

No one knew where this tunnel would lead. Pip told Meg and the others not to make a sound. Then he moved ahead cautiously, peeping around each corner. A little farther along they came to another bend. Pip inched forward until he saw a sinister figure through the gloom. Coming towards him in the ghostly light was Chark!

The short-tailed shrew was muttering to himself as he snuffled along. Pip knew that the slightest scratch from Chark's red-tipped teeth meant death. But turning back was also out of the question. Pip's heart beat wildly as he tried to think what to do.

Just then one of the younger mice spotted the shrew and squeaked in fright. Chark heard the cry and rose on his hind legs. Peering short-sightedly down the tunnel, he swayed to and fro as he tried to locate the sound. Pip noticed how unsteady Chark was on his feet. That gave him an idea. It was a dangerous gamble, but it just might work.

Summoning his courage, Pip signalled to Meg and the others to

follow. Then he charged down the passage, butted Chark in the stomach, and bowled him over. Flat on his back, Chark flailed the air like a beetle, while Pip and his party ran by on either side. By the time the shrew got back on his feet, the mice were gone. Chark gnashed his teeth and squealed with rage.

The mice pelted along the tunnel until they finally came to an exit. When they emerged into the sunlight, they were only a short distance from the hedge. Quickly they split up and went home. Meg and Pip waited until everyone was safely on his way, then scurried to Meg's den.

Meg's winter burrow was in the centre of an ancient pile of rocks surrounded by hawthorn bushes that acted as prickly umbrellas to keep out hawks and owls. It had several rooms, and it was well stocked with food.

While Meg and Pip feasted on hawberries and apple seeds, they relived the events of the day, mourning the mice that had died and marvelling at their own narrow escapes.

"Your mother was right about the bluebird, Pip," Meg exclaimed. "You really are a lucky mouse!"

All of a sudden, Meg changed the subject. "Who do you think will lead the deer-mouse community now that Pero is gone?"

"Well, it certainly won't be me," Pip said. "Remember, I'm an outsider."

"But, Pip, you were the one who sounded the warning in the chamber, and you were the one who led us to safety."

"Meg, there's no way the other mice would accept me."

"We'll see, Pip, but as far as I'm concerned, you're the one who should be leader."

They fell silent for a few minutes. Nervously Pip began to play with an apple seed, turning it over and over in his paws.

"You know, Meg, we've been through a lot together, and I think we have a special bond." He paused.

"Yes, Pip."

"You've been my best friend."

Again Pip paused, rotating the apple seed in his paws. This time the shiny brown seed fell to the ground.

Meg picked it up. "Pip, what are you trying to say?"

Pip shifted uncomfortably from one haunch to the other. Finally he blurted it out. "What I'm trying to say, Meg, is ... is ... will you be my mate?"

Meg nestled up to him. "Of course I will."

The two mice began their life together in Meg's winter den. As soon as the weather got a bit warmer, they planned to move aboveground to a summer home.

One evening The Gapper dropped by. Pip and Meg were delighted to have their old friend the red-backed vole as their first visitor.

"I heard the crows talking the other day," The Gapper said. "Apparently the mouse community has elected a new leader."

"Did they say who it is?" asked Meg.

"No, no, they didn't say. You can't believe the crows, anyway. They're such gossips."

The Gapper seemed to be in a hurry. "I've got a lot to do, a lot to do," he said and continued on his way.

As he scurried along the hedge, Pip and Meg heard The Gapper chuckling to himself. "Won't they be surprised. Surprised indeed!"

After he disappeared, they sat side by side on a smooth rock and watched the moon come up. The night was warm, and spring was in the air. In a little while they would forage in the field, but for now they were content to sit together quietly.

Soon Pip noticed a deer mouse coming towards them along the hedge. Meg saw another approaching from the opposite direction. Then three appeared from the field. More than a dozen mice eventually gathered in front of them.

Pip didn't know what to make of it. But he didn't have to wait long to find out. After some whispering, an adult stepped forward. Pip recognized him as one of those he had led to safety.

"Pip, we came to thank you for saving us from the foxes and Chark." The mouse drummed his front paws for a moment. "And we're sorry for shunning you and Meg."

Pip was at a loss for words.

"We've also come to ask a special favour. We've talked it over, and we would like you to be our new leader."

The mice waited anxiously for his answer.

"I'd be honoured," Pip replied. "But from now on, there will be no more insiders and outsiders. Everyone will be welcome in our community."

The other mice squeaked with approval and pressed forward to congratulate him.

Meg beamed at Pip. "I told you so," she whispered.

In early May, Pip cleared out the den he had used the previous summer. Meg, expecting her first litter, lined the space under the fallen limb with the softest grasses. Outside, purple violets peeped through the withered leaves, and wild strawberries unfolded their white petals in the sun.

Meg's three babies were born a few weeks later, and Pip, like all deer-mouse fathers, moved to another home. But he visited his family as often as he could. As the days sped by, the babies became more and more curious. Pip, remembering his own childhood, taught them the dangers of the field and the forest.

He had never been happier. As he dozed in his nest in the apple tree, he remembered being orphaned and the long, hot trip on

the train. He thought of his narrow escape from Trutta, and the harsh reception Pero had given him. The feeling of not belonging. The overwhelming loneliness.

But all that was behind him. He was now the leader of the mouse community, he had Meg and three babies. Just thinking about his good fortune made him want to see his family.

Meg heard Pip singing as he came along the hedge, and poked her head out of the entrance to her den. "What are you so happy about?" she asked.

"Oh, just that I'm the luckiest mouse in the world," Pip replied.

They looked at each other for a moment, then happily touched noses.